StoneSoup

*The magazine supporting
creative kids around the world*

Editor
Emma Wood

Director
William Rubel

Operations
Jane Levi

Education & Production
Sarah Ainsworth

Design
Joe Ewart

Stone Soup (ISSN 0094 579X) is published 11 times per year—monthly, with a combined July/August summer issue. Copyright © 2019 by the Children's Art Foundation, a 501(c)(3) nonprofit organization located in Santa Cruz, California. All rights reserved.

Thirty-five percent of our subscription price is tax-deductible. Make a donation at Stonesoup.com/donate, and support us by choosing Children's Art Foundation as your Amazon Smile charity.

POSTMASTER: Send address changes to Stone Soup, 126 Otis Street, Santa Cruz, CA 95060. Periodicals postage paid at Santa Cruz, California, and additional offices.

Stone Soup is available in different formats to persons who have trouble seeing or reading the print or online editions. To request the Braille edition from the National Library of Congress, call +1 800-424-8567. To request access to the audio edition via the National Federation of the Blind's NFB-NEWSLINE®, call +1 866-504-7300 or visit www.nfbnewsline.org.

Check us out on social media:

Editor's Note

Often, the work in our issues is just as concerned with animals and the natural world as with humanity and civilization—not by choice, but by necessity: it reflects our contributors' interests. But, in this issue, people and civilization (cities! cars! castles!) are the main subjects. Patrick Lusa's poem "Numbers" captures the hustle and bustle of everyday life; Anna Shepherd's story "Twenty Questions, Twenty Answers" explores the complicated-but-close relationship between two sisters; and Mia Fang's digital portrait "Lady in the Willows by the River" (on the cover) places a person squarely in the center of our usual cover landscape.

We hope you enjoy reading and looking at the many other works that appear in this issue, and that you leave feeling inspired to send us some people- and car-filled stories, poetry, and artwork.

Letters: We love to hear from our readers. Please post a comment on our website or write to us via Submittable or editor@stonesoup. com. Your letter might be published on our occasional Letters to the Editor page.

Submissions: Our guidelines are on the Submit page at Stonesoup.com, where you will also find a link to our Submittable online submissions portal.

Subscriptions: To subscribe to *Stone Soup*, please press the Subscribe button on our web page, Stonesoup.com.

On the cover:
"Lady in the Willows by the River"

**by Mia Fang, 13
West Lafayette, IN**

StoneSoup
Contents

ART

PORTRAITS: A MULTI-ARTIST PORTFOLIO

Bird in the Clouds, *Nikon Coolpix L830*

by Hannah Parker, 13
South Burlington, VT

Twenty Questions, Twenty Answers

by Anna Shepherd, 11
Brooklyn, NY

*An infuriating game of twenty questions pushes
Jenny to scour her childhood memories*

Only ten minutes had gone by since the last rest stop, but to me it felt like an hour. My knee bounced. My leg jiggled. My fingers drummed out syncopated rhythms on the door handle.

"*Jennifer,*" said my older sister, Ula, "stop tapping."

I gritted my teeth and began slapping the side of my thigh instead. "It's Jenny."

"*Jennifer*, you're still making noise."

"My name is Jenny!"

"Ula, Jenny, stop bickering," said Mom in that stiff, controlled voice that meant she was trying very, very hard not to yell. "Especially you, Ula. You're 15. You should know better."

Dad turned around in the passenger seat. "Girls, you're stressing her out. Why don't you play Twenty Questions?"

"Yes," I said instantly. Ula groaned, but I noticed the look of satisfaction in her brown eyes.

"I'll start," she said in a practiced drawl.

"Fine."

The car fell silent while Ula thought of her object. I stared out the window at the wall of leafy green trees parading down the side of the road, bars of Mozart and Seitz and Boccherini running through my head. My own face—straight, thick black hair framing yellow-hazel eyes—looked dispassionately back at me. After a while, I switched to thinking about strange things that could happen as a result of insufficient AI attempts: *A self-driving car is driving down a road. A tree falls across the road, and the car drives into it and explodes. However, right before it explodes, the car sends a record of what has happened to all the other self-driving cars. Instead of concluding that you should stop if a tree falls across the road, the cars all conclude that you should not drive near trees.* I smiled at the image of cars inexplicably avoiding large swathes of forest.

"All right," Ula announced. "I'm ready." *Finally*, I thought, turning from the window. My sister's eyes were narrowed, as if in challenge. Her curly blonde hair had frizzed up around her face, making her look like some sort of evil villain in a comic book.

"Is it a vegetable?"

"No."

Ugh. Already I just felt like lying

down and going to sleep. "Is it an animal?"

She hesitated. "No." The word seemed drawn-out, uncertain. That caught my attention. Ula was never unsure of something in Twenty Questions—or any game, for that matter. At least, she never showed it.

"Is it a mineral?" I almost asked, but caught myself. Since there were only three categories—vegetable, animal, or mineral—it had to be. Furious at my mistake, I took a deep breath and said, "Is it bigger than a bread box?"

"No."

"Is it a sort of big rock?"

"A *small boulder*. No."

"Is it a regular object?"

"No."

"Can it be seen if I look outside?"

"No."

I hated how calm she was, how robotic, how unfazed by my questions. If this were a battle, I thought, she'd be winning.

"Have we seen it before?"

"Yes."

I blurted out the first question that came to my mouth. "When was the last time we saw it?"

Ula's mouth curled into a mocking sneer. "That's not a yes-or-no question."

I gritted my teeth.

"And it counts."

"Was the last time we saw it more than one year ago?"

"Yes."

"More than two?"

"Yes."

"More than three?"

"Yes."

"More than four?"

"No."

So when I was seven.

Okay, this was not fair. But I knew I couldn't back down now.

I cast my memory back to important things that had happened four years ago. That was the year Dad had hurt his foot, leaving him unable to drive and with a limp. And the thing he had dropped on his foot was . . .

Oh. The Christmas tree.

Which would be classified in the vegetable category.

I searched for other things, and my mind was drawn to a sweltering July day in Washington, D.C. Ula and I had had identical dripping raspberry gelato cones, which we licked desperately as we wandered with our parents around Capitol Hill. Despite my efforts, my hands and face had been glazed with bright red liquid.

We had walked through Eastern Market, and even though I saw the same thing every day, I had been mesmerized by all the crazy kinds of produce for sale. The gelato on my face and hands somewhat mopped up, I had gingerly felt the scales of an artichoke, nervously prodded a pineapple's serrated leaves, and generously tasted every plate of fruit samples, stopping only when my parents (and Ula) had dragged me away with angry scolding.

Then, at Ula's and my plaintive requests, we had gone to the library, with its blissfully cool aisles of bookshelves and its little reading tables by the windows. I had plopped down at one of them with a foot-high stack of *Magic Tree House* books I knew I wouldn't be able to finish while Ula prowled the shelves.

We had left the library and continued down the sweltering street. Ula and I had run back and forth along the red-bricked sidewalk, gathering up handfuls of fallen flowers from the crape myrtles and presenting them—I more proudly than Ula—to our parents. Secretly, I had swiped several sprigs of mint from a thick clump growing in someone's front yard and peeking through the black-painted fence, thinking to use it for tea later.

Something about that blissful day, so full of possibilities, so free of obligations, felt important. But nothing about it had anything to do with minerals. Reluctantly, I shifted the focus of my mental metal detector.

Soon, it felt as if I had gone through every memory I had of the year 2014. There was my birthday in August—a water fight at Lincoln Park, with high-velocity squirt guns and hundreds of water balloons. And Ula's in March, spent holed up inside our not-exactly-gigantic apartment with ten preteens who were antsy from eating too much candy. There was the first day of school, the last day of school, the time I won the math competition, the time Ula won the chess camp tournament, and the time I won the vocabulary word fashion show. (I won it the year after that, too.) There was the day Ula had held a funeral for the nest of baby mice we'd found starved to death in the wall of our house—which the rest of us only participated in because Mom and Dad felt obliged to encourage Ula's love for nature and animals, and I felt guilty and rude to be the only person in the family not attending. There was moving day, when we moved from our old apartment into a bigger one two blocks away. That was a terrible day for everyone, because not only was it drizzling the yucky kind of lukewarm summer rain but the moment we left our apartment building some construction workers came by and bulldozed it flat.

"Um, is it the bulldozer?"

"The *what*?"

"Never mind."

"It counts."

I sighed. Suddenly, I thought of something. "Is it that statue in Lincoln Park?"

"No, and by that way, we see that almost every day."

I groaned. This was kind of like thinking you could fly, jumping off the roof of a building, going splat on the sidewalk three stories below, and then waking up in the hospital and wondering why the heck you thought you could fly in the first place.

I leaned back in my seat and closed my eyes. This drive was taking so long.

If only we could get to Aunt Megan's house. Then I wouldn't have to bother finishing this stupid game. I squeezed my eyes tighter, trying to recall what she looked like. Red hair, piled up on top of her head in a sort of beehive . . . or was I thinking of Grandma in those old photos?

Definitely Grandma.

Anyway, this wasn't my fault. I hadn't seen my aunt and cousins, or their house in Upstate New York, for several years. Not since I turned—

I sat bolt upright in my seat. I could almost feel the light bulb going off in my head. I shut my eyes again. Wasn't Aunt Megan's house on a lake?

"Is it the lake Aunt Megan's house is on?"

Ula narrowed her eyes at me. "Aunt Megan's house isn't on a lake. Gramps's is. And . . ."

"*That counts*," I finished under my breath.

With a jolt, I realized I was at 15. Only five questions left. I made a growling noise deep in my throat. *Why does Ula have to win at everything?* But I also knew, somewhere inside me, that I was too interested at this point to give up. I desperately wanted to know what this object was.

I took a deep breath.

I will do this. I would show her.

Think, my brain commanded. And so I went back to my only lead—that summer day, spent wandering our home.

"Please, can we see the cherry blossoms?" Ula had begged. And my parents had given their consent, even though it was much too late for cherry blossoms, because we had all known

that Ula would find beauty in even the saddest, brownest, most wilted handful of flowers.

We had boarded a train on the subway, heading to the Mall. We had gotten off at our stop and climbed the steps to the surface again, emerging into the hot, too-bright sunlight. The Washington Monument had risen, blindingly white, in front of us.

I loved that part of the city. Everything was in various shades of white, cream, and beige—even the sidewalks. My seven-year-old self had looked down at the ground, which was made up of light-brown gravel that was getting in my worn red sandals. I had been reminded for some reason of the pebbles sunken into the ground in front of CHAW (Capitol Hill Arts Workshop).

I blinked. Turned to Ula. "Is it your favorite CHAW pebble?"

"My what?"

"The blue pebble. Next to the *C* in CHAW. You know, where it spells out CHAW in the concrete. In front of CHAW." *Stop rambling*, I told myself.

"Oh. That. No."

Four questions left.

By the time we had reached the cherry blossoms, we were sweating profusely, despite having stayed in the shade the entire way there. While Ula danced among the drooping, slightly shriveled trees, picking up every fallen flower she could find, I had looked sleepily across the Tidal Basin. Only a few boats had bobbed in the water, and I had been glad that I wasn't in one of them. Briefly, I wondered if Ula's object was a boat, then just as quickly dismissed the idea. Last year, I remembered, we had ridden on one ourselves.

Another thought crossed my mind. Recklessly, I asked, "Is it a cloudless sky?"

Ula snorted. "The last time I saw a cloudless sky was before I was born."

"That's not—"

"In other words, cloudless skies are nonexistent."

"What an optimistic thing to say."

"If I were an optimist, my life would suck. I would be disappointed by everything."

I ignored her and plunged back into the vivid waters of my memories. I had been startled out of my drowsy haze by Ula's voice crying out. "What is it, Ula?" Mom had asked, a trace of worry in her voice.

"Mom. Dad. Jenny." Ula had sounded as if she were crying.

"What is it?" I had called, overcome with worry and sympathy for my big sister.

"Look." When we had raced over, we had seen a baby sparrow lying on the ground underneath one of the cherry trees, its left wing broken. It was dead.

"Help me bury it," Ula had pleaded. When my parents were reluctant, she had snapped, "Well, then I'm taking it home and doing it myself!"

"If you bury it here, you have to do it by yourself," Mom had said.

"Fine!"

After what had seemed like forever, Ula was done. She had even found a small, gravestone-like rock to place on top. We had listened to her short speech in honor of the bird, and then Dad had suggested heading back home. Everyone had readily agreed.

No sooner had we turned onto our street than clouds suddenly swept over the sun and rain came pouring down. By the time we reached the door, we had been drenched.

And then suddenly it hit me. It was so simple, so obvious, and so devilishly Ula . . .

"Is it water?"

"If we hadn't seen water in four years, we'd be dead."

"Oh." Suddenly I felt so idiotic, like I did whenever I played chess.

And I had two questions left.

This is hopeless . . .

For the first time, I just felt like giving up. I could give two half-hearted guesses, let Ula reveal the answer, and the whole thing would be over. I wouldn't have to bother with any of this. I wouldn't have to try anymore.

After all, it's just a game.

"Is it a brick?"

"No."

"Is it . . . "

I trailed off as we pulled into a driveway. Looking out the window, I saw a two-story house with an attic, painted a bright, cheerful yellow. There wasn't a lake in sight.

"We're here," Mom announced.

I let out a sigh of relief. *Safe.* Gratefully, I reached for the door handle. But

But just as my fingers grasped the warm metal, something clicked in my head.

Love Stone, *iPhone*

by Tatiana Hadzic, 11
New York, NY

just as my fingers grasped the warm metal, something clicked in my head.

A mineral. Smaller than a bread box. Irregular shape. The more I thought about it, the more sure I was that I was right. For once, everything fit.

I turned around. Ula was still in the car. I said to her, "It's the rock that you put on the sparrow's grave." Then, wanting to share my brilliant revelation with someone, I added, "You hesitated when I asked if it was an animal because you weren't sure if you wanted to make it the sparrow itself. That's why."

Ula was now opening her door. With her back to me, she said, "No."

I gaped. "What?"

"I said no. I don't choose stupid things like that. You're wrong. I win." She opened the door and got out of the car.

Desperately, I called after her, "Then what is it?"

Ula's voice floated faintly back to me. "I don't have to tell you if I don't want to."

"But—"

"It's just a game. It doesn't matter anyway."

"Yes, it does!"

She ignored me.

Stunned, I watched through my window as my parents and Ula headed for the door, dragging our luggage. I could see my cousins Cecily and Emma pushing the door open now, with Aunt Megan behind them. Her hair was the color of her house.

"You're lying," I said to no one.

I had been right. I was sure of it.

A Magnificent City

by Ziqing (Izzie) Peng, 10
Nanjing, China

Something beautiful for us might be poisonous for others

I'm living in a magnificent city. In the morning, when the first sunlight illuminates the earth, the buildings seem to wear a beautiful yarn shirt. The world revives, people get to work. Cars make a beautiful picture, like a glittering lake.

In the afternoon, flowers blossom, trees and grass make a marvelous photo. Children play happily. There's laughter everywhere.

In the evening, colorful lights open. The city looks like the dark sky with shining stars. The wind blows. Slowly, the city becomes quiet. All the lives are sleeping. The lively city becomes mysterious and poetic. Everything is sleeping except the lights. They change every second to make magnificent pictures. They light the sky and make night into morning.

But the magnificent lights also cause problems. Some small turtles are born on the beach, and they need to go back to the sea. They only know that the sea is light and take the city as the sea because the city is much lighter than the sea. When they miss their way, they may die.

So not every magnificent city is good for wildlife. Something beautiful for us might be poisonous for others.

Cranes and Christmas Tree, *Canon Rebel T4i*

by Nicholas Taplitz, 13
Los Angeles, CA

Numbers

by Patrick Lusa, 11
Stafford Springs, CT

1 winter day at
2 in the morning there are
3 people sleeping as
4 owls are hooting before they go to sleep at
5 a.m.
6 in the morning and the owls have stopped hooting,
7 birds are chirping as they search for food.
8 dogs are barking,
9 cats are hissing as they fight at
10 in the morning, there are
11 people driving to lunch at
12.
13 days later, there is heat again.
14 people are swimming in the
15-mile lake.
16 cars are driving to exit
17, taking people to work.
18 days have passed now
19 people are in school getting bored to death.
20 people are running the
21-mile race.
22 days later, the heat is getting stronger,
On the 23rd, days are getting longer.
The world seems to turn faster.
The racers run faster.
The light is still putting up a fight.
24 hours after midnight.

The Sky

The sky seems endless.
All of the birds fly in it.
The huge blue abyss.

Shadow in the Sun, *gouache and acrylic*

by Isha Narang, 13
Austin, TX

Two Princes

by Lia Taylor, 12
Elkins Park, PA

When his father, the king, asks him to choose a wife, Prince Richard realizes he can't marry a woman

Once there was a beautiful kingdom called Galavor. Giant trees and impossibly green grass flooded the land like a smile on a baby's face. The sun would always shine without a doubt, warming the vast kingdom. The king, King Charle, seemed reasonable and fair. His dark, stiff beard and squinty eyes created a wise and trustworthy appeal. Everyone was happy and everyone adored their ruler.

One warm June day, King Charle and his only child, Prince Richard, were eating a breakfast of omelettes and fresh fruit. They ate alone, as the Queen had passed away a few years prior, and all of Richard's brothers had passed away at a young age. As per usual, the only noise was clinking cutlery. Prince Richard's soft, platinum-blond hair occasionally fell into his emerald green eyes. His hands almost blended in with the porcelain chinaware. He was in premium health, but his complexion matched his mother's, at least in his last memory of her. His bony body made the prince appear puny, but he was stronger and nobler than any man within the kingdom.

Suddenly, King Charle broke the silence. "Son, while I hope to live much longer, we do have to acknowledge that I am getting older. In two months' time, you will turn 21, and by then you shall be engaged to the woman of your choosing. Then you and your fiancée will get married and have a coronation, for it is an event I wish to be present for. Today, you shall travel to the next kingdom, Spañia, to search for a wife."

"While I do not disagree with you, Father, I would like to ask: why you are planning to step down from the throne so early in your life? You are only 60 years of age. You must remember, I am your youngest child, as my brothers have long passed. But, very well. If that is what you wish, I must obey. I will pack after breakfast," responded Richard.

"Very well," said King Charle. The men continued to eat in silence.

At about noon, when the sun was high in the sky, Richard mounted his black stallion, gave a small wave to his father, and set off on his two-day journey to Spañia. About two hours into his ride, he began to think about what he searched for in a wife. Romantic, independent, strong . . . As he tried to picture his perfect bride, he realized that each time he imagined her, she wasn't the slim, graceful woman that is thought to be the most beautiful. Instead, she was more handsome than pretty and had a sturdy build. He realized that marrying and starting a family with a woman filled his heart with dread. He only wished to befriend women. He thought he was starting to hallucinate. So, after only three hours, he stopped for a nap beneath a willow tree.

He arrived at the palace of Spañia around two o'clock in the afternoon, when the kingdom was at its hottest. The palace was built at the top of a tall, brown, and rocky cliff. While Spañia was just as beautiful as Galavor, it was pretty in a different way. It was warm and mystical. The royal family greeted him at the gate: King Ferdinand, Queen Isabel, Princess Isabel (the eldest sister), Princess Mia (the youngest sister), and Prince Francisco. They were all kind and very welcoming. While Isabel was the prettiest of the princesses, Mia took the most interest in Richard right away. Richard knew picking a bride would be difficult, especially considering he was attracted to neither of them. Instead, he took a strong interest in the prince, Francisco.

Lucky for Richard, it was Francisco who showed him around the palace and helped to get him settled in his room, which was between Princess Isabel's room and Francisco's room. As Richard put his things away, he noticed the massive and beautiful garden outside his window.

At six o'clock, dinner was served. Richard was placed between Isabel and Mia, and across from Francisco. The King and Queen sat at either end of the long, rectangular table. Throughout the evening, Richard had boring, two-sentence conversations with both princesses. ("How was the trip?" "Fine." Or, "The salmon is quite delicious." "Yes, it really is.") Finally, Richard remembered the garden.

"I couldn't help but notice the beautiful garden you have here," said Prince Richard.

"Ah, yes," said Francisco. "I love it. It's where I spend most of my time. If I'm not gardening, I'm wandering, or reading under a willow tree. But, really, it's nothing much. If you like, Richard, I can show you after dinner?"

While Richard's hair fell in his face, he wondered what it would be like to have Francisco's dark complexion and stiff, yet wavy, black hair. He was the most attractive man he had ever seen. He liked his kindness too. He admired how humble he was.

"Of course! That would be fantastic!" Richard exclaimed.

"Great. I'll meet you in your room at 7:30," decided Francisco.

At 7:32, Richard was still waiting in his bedroom, which was quite luxurious. He was starting to worry. "What if he has forgotten?" he thought. "Maybe I should go check on Francisco, to remind him of our—" Richard was not sure how to define it—"date?" Richard thought it was a date, but did Francisco? Did Richard want it to be a date? Richard was now more nervous than ever. As he stood to check on the prince, there was a short and rhythmic knock at the door.

"Richard? Sorry I'm late. Are you ready?" called the voice of Francisco, through the door.

"I'll be right out, and don't be sorry, it's alright," replied Richard. A second later, the two men stood together in the corridor. Richard found Francisco especially dashing. Was this a date? It seemed the answer was yes. To his own surprise, Richard smiled at the revelation.

"Shall we?" Francisco put out his arm. Richard reluctantly rested his hand atop Francisco's arm. He didn't *want* to want to, but he did. What was this new feeling? Was it . . . attraction? This was something he had never felt before. He never thought he would fall for anyone, especially a *prince*.

Back home, Richard had never met anybody who was gay. It was not allowed, because his father, King Charle, had made a law against same-sex couples. If they were found out, they would be banished. Richard never understood this, but everyone knows better than to question a king's judgement. Richard wasn't in Galavor now, though.

Francisco led Richard through the gardens. As they walked, Francisco started a bouquet of his favorites, the flowers he nurtured the most. A white rose, an orchid, a tiger lily, a peony. After two hours of laughs and banter, the bouquet had grown full. Francisco gently placed the flowers into Richard's hands. There was a silence, but not awkward. They each gazed into each other's eyes.

"I don't want to marry either of your sisters," said Richard. His pale cheeks turned bright red with embarrassment. The contrast made him look even paler.

"I know that. If you were to marry them then why would you be here, on a date with me? You . . . you do know this is a date, right?" Francisco seemed confused. "You came here to find a fiancé; I thought you had chosen me."

"Umm, no . . . I don't know. My father wouldn't approve. We could never inherit the kingdom . . . " mumbled Richard.

"We'll figure it out. A happy kingdom needs happy rulers. I know you don't like my sisters, so—be with me?"

"I- I don't know. My father is a scary man." Richard took a deep breath, inhaling the thick scent of his bouquet. The bouquet that Francisco had given him. Francisco, the only person he could clearly and fondly see in his future. "Okay, but we need a plan, for our future."

"Isabel and Mia, they are just magnificent with secrets. They never intended on marrying you anyway. They'll be in the study"

The four stayed up all night suggesting ideas. Overthrowing Galavor would not be popular among citizens. Isabel was next in line to rule if Francisco was unable, and she intended to take that chance. Many ideas were proposed, all shot down.

"What if you founded your own kingdom?" proposed Isabel.

"You could run away, take Pegasus," added Mia.

"Anyone from Spañia or Galavor could come with us, to be citizens of a new land," suggested Francisco.

"Yes! This could work! We'll lead on Pegasus with our citizens in boats below," Richard exclaimed.

"And King Charle will never have to know. We'll work by night," Mia explained.

"No, no. He needs to know. I will confront him tomorrow. May I take Pegasus? My horse is ill, and it will make traveling faster," said Richard.

"Of course!" said Isabel.

Pegasus was a large white mare with a wingspan longer than a man is tall. Gentle in nature, yet strong at heart. Richard climbed aboard cautiously, but soon realized he was perfectly safe, and the draining two-day trip became an exhilarating two hours. It filled the timid and confused prince with confidence.

As Pegasus started her descent to the castle grounds, Richard noticed the king waiting patiently outside the castle.

"Hello, Richard, have you found a fiancée?" asked King Charle.

"Yes, I have." Richard said this confidently, yet inside he was dreading the moment.

"And her name?" prompted the king.

" . . . Francisco. His name is Francisco," said Prince Richard, sheepishly. And with that, he took off, back to Spañia, feeling a mix of emotions. Brave, proud, worried. He had fled before his father even had time to react.

A few days later, everything was ready for the escape. Richard was overjoyed that he could spend his life with the one he loved so dearly, but there was the familiar emptiness of loss, an emptiness he hadn't felt since the death of his mother.

Flying, the two princes could see everything for miles and miles, including the large ship of hopeful citizens. Then, somebody below shouted "Land ho!" A loud cheering erupted, then quickly faded as they saw the state of the land. Death flooded the landscape. Ashes and dead grass spread as far as the eye could see. The joy melted from people's faces. Nevertheless, Richard and Francisco guided Pegasus to the ground. As they landed, the ship was pushed up onto the shore.

Everyone was uneasy, except for their leaders. The princes felt the earth calling to them, begging to be nourished and lived on.

In unison, the princes announced, "Behold, our new kingdom! We shall call it Terracinis! We will create life upon this ashy land. We will live with the land, not on it. We will find beauty in this demolished plain." They said this with such confidence and hope that the people were able to understand.

The land appreciated this and became beautiful right before their eyes. The grass was greener than grass should be, but was undeniably healthy. The air was fresh and the flowers could bring tears to eyes with their exquisite beauty. The land saw the hope and love in the hearts of the princes and gave them sweet fruit, in ample amounts. A crystal palace rose from the ground and a sweet, quaint village swirled up from the ashes. Birds placed crowns fit for a king onto the heads of the princes.

"Long live the kings!" cheered the crowd of citizens, awestruck and joyful. The people of Terracinis lived happily ever after.

Portraits: A Multi-Artist Portfolio

Editor's Note

In visual art, a portrait is traditionally a painting, drawing, or photograph that depicts a person's face. Before photography was invented in the 1800s, people would usually commission portraits of their friends and family so as to have an image of the person they loved. Important and wealthy individuals—like the monarchs in Europe—might have many portraits painted of them throughout their lifetime. But a middle-class person might only have one or two. And someone in the lower class—perhaps none. So, for a long time, a portrait was associated with status. Today, a photographic portrait is cheap: you can get your best friend to take a professional-looking photo of you with your phone on 'portrait' mode. But, because of the time and skill required, the painted portrait still remains rare.

An excellent portrait is not necessarily the one that most accurately or realistically portrays its subject; it is the one that somehow captures the subject's inner being—that gives the viewer some sense of who that person is, not just what they look like.

In this portfolio of portraits, four different artists are exploring the form in their own unique ways. By using a variety of materials to make up the face in her portrait, Sritanvee Alluri emphasizes how each of us is composed of different pieces of the world: of what we read, hear, watch, and think. In her two portraits, Amalia Ichilov uses soft, visible brushstrokes to create a more realistic—yet somewhat dreamy—representation of her subjects, who appear refreshingly 'normal', like someone you could run into on the street. Using Autodesk Sketchbook, a drawing and painting software, Leo Melinsky has turned his attention not to people but to dogs—and succeeds in capturing their personalities: Ernie—standing, mouth closed, looking off the page—appears high-strung and hyper-alert, waiting perhaps for someone to throw his ball, whereas Hazel—drooling, sitting, relaxed—seems easygoing. Finally, Isabella Webb, in painting Queen Elizabeth II, reminds us of the history of portraiture, with an image that captures the Queen's friendly-but-always-formal attitude.

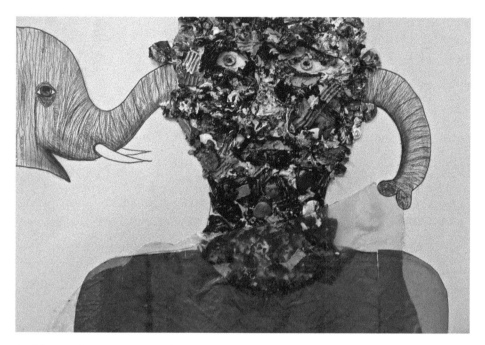

In Through One Ear and Out the Other, *mixed media*

by Sritanvee Alluri, 12
Austin, TX

Portrait of a Woman Standing Against a Blue Wall, *oil pastel on paper*

Portrait of a Freckled Young Woman, *oil pastel on paper*

by Amalia Ichilov, 9
New York, NY

Ernie, *Autodesk Sketchbook*

by Leo Melinsky, 12
Clayton, NC

Hazel, *Autodesk Sketchbook*

The Queen, *oil paint*

by Isabella Webb, 11
Berkshire, UK

Gone Fishing

by Mia Fang, 13
West Lafayette, IN

When Lily's father loses his job, he enlists in the army to support his family

Chapter 1

I lay on my bed, wracked with worry. Horrible thoughts floated on my conscience. I buried my face in my pillow, my long hair spread over the silk. I tried pushing the thoughts away, with no luck. It was hard concentrating on anything these days. I had pushed my friends away, and spent less and less time with my mother. I knew she was worried too, but I had to admit I was angry. I play the scene over and over again in my head: why did it have to be my family to suffer?

A month ago, my life couldn't have been more perfect. I had sat at the table waiting for Father to come home. Wonderful smells rose from the pot of stew. Cloves of dried garlic and mushrooms hung from the ceiling. The light of the setting sun seeped through the window, casting a warm glow on the kitchen. I watched as the soft figure of Mother stirred in herbs and spices, her long, strawberry-blonde hair flowing down her back. Like Father, I had a head full of flame-red hair and a face swarming with freckles.

Mother was 18 weeks pregnant and her stomach was really starting to swell; I couldn't imagine what it would be like to have a sibling, if Father would love him or her more than me.

Soon, the front door swung open with a creak and the tall figure of Father stood in the doorway. He set his bag down with a heavy thud and hung up his hat and scarf. He walked in, shaking the snow from his hair without speaking. It wasn't like him. He sat down wearily as if the weight of the world was resting on his shoulders. I ran up and hugged him, clinging to the plush arm of the chair. I looked into his eyes, which seemed more tired than usual. He gave me a small smile and playfully rubbed my hair, though his smile faltered and a grim expression took its place.

"Holly," he said, turning to Mother. "I have some bad news to share with you and Lily."

Mother turned around calm as ever, and slowly sat down next to Father. Her presence was reassuring.

I sat quietly and listened, a bad feeling creeping up my gut. But I wasn't afraid then. Mother had that effect on people.

"It's my job," Father said, looking

down. "I got laid off today. I'm to collect my last paycheck tomorrow." He looked up at us. "I'm really sorry. I s-should have tried harder."

Mother and I, we wrapped our arms around Father, unsure of what to think or of what lay ahead.

I laid in bed staring at my wallpaper: bright colors beamed from my walls, fields of livid flowers, a small cottage bordered in a white picket fence. My eyelids felt heavy. Worried whispers floated through the floorboards.

That Sunday I woke up to warm smells coming from the kitchen. I walked down the stairs, floorboards squeaking under my feet. Father stood grinning with an apron tied around his waist.

"Morning, sunshine!" he called and placed a bowl of oats in front of me.

"Where's Mother?" I asked.

"She wasn't feeling up to it this morning. She's in her room right now. I think it would be wise to leave her alone for right now."

That's not like her, I thought. Mother was a put together, down-to-earth woman, and was always the calm one. I wondered what was upsetting her so much.

"Don't worry too much, Lily. I was thinking we could go fishing today, just the two of us. We will have to stop by town to get some bait before we head off, though."

We walked into town. I was dressed in a plain, light blue Sunday dress with a Peter Pan collar. It's a nice dress, but not my best by far. It was perfect for a day of fishing.

We walked down the cobblestone streets. I walked slightly behind Father. His tall figure perfectly hid me from the crowds. I slouched, keeping my head down, hoping to make myself seem smaller and less noticeable. I'm a shy girl, and talking to strangers was never my thing. Mother always told me how much I was like my father, but in my opinion we couldn't have been more different. I watched as Father tipped his hat to a gentleman walking by with a polite "How do you do?" I cringed just thinking of a social interactions, and felt more grateful than ever for Father's protective shadow.

We loaded our little rowboat on a lake with our bait, fishing poles and lunches. Here on the lake, there was a peaceful silence, away from the crowds and people. Away from the vendors and markets. I felt safe here. It was Father's and my special place here, where we had come so often. I climbed into the gently rocking boat and straightened my posture.

Father rowed the boat off the shore, the paddles breaking the water's surface, sending ripples out on the emerald lake. Fog spread across the lake, weaving its tendrils over the still waters. The outlines of faraway moun-

Only two months, I thought, then Father will be back.

tains were barely visible, green with all the lush vegetation. I breathed in the fresh air, smelling hints of pine and the familiar earthy smell. Ancient evergreens and willows stood tall along the shore watching over us like guardians.

Father cast his line, and I followed shortly after. We sat like that in a silence for a while and, after an hour with no catches, he turned to me.

"Lily, you know we have a beautiful big house with a stove and three stories, but anything beautiful costs money."

I loved our house, decked with its colorful wallpapers, its big windows, and spiral staircases.

"Well," Father said. "Since I lost my job, it will be hard to keep our house and pay taxes. The bank might evict us if we don't get payments in soon."

"Will we have to move?" I asked. "I don't want to!" *That was our home, and for the bank to take it would be so unfair!*

"Yeah, I figured you wouldn't want to," he said with a chuckle. "I found a new job that will support our family."

"That's so great! What kind of job is it?"

"I'm going into the military."

Chapter 2
Anger and Guilt

I sat looking out my window without seeing. *Only two months*, I thought, *then Father will be back.* They had stationed him in Russia to fight in the Second World War.

When he left, I began noticing how big of a hole he left in our fami-ly. Walking into the master bedroom with only one side of the bed occupied. Hoping for him to magically walk through our door. Suddenly, I began noticing his scent everywhere—on the laundry hung out to dry, on the couches and chairs. My heart ached for his presence, and I knew Mother wasn't doing much better, but that didn't stop me from thinking horrible thoughts I know I shouldn't.

Why couldn't Mother get a job? Then Father would still be here. Why couldn't she help out the family more?

But as soon as those thoughts entered my mind, I felt a wave of guilt. It wasn't her fault. But thoughts are addictive, dangerous, contagious.

Mother knocked at my door. "Supper's ready, sweetie."

I didn't answer. I heard her footsteps descending the stairs. I felt a wave of homesickness even though I was at home. I flopped down on my bed and slowly drifted off to sleep.

When I awoke, the sun had set and moonlight sent shafts of light in my bedroom. I felt a dull pain in my stomach, hunger. I walked downstairs and wondered if Mother was still up, but found the kitchen empty. My bowl of soup was still on the table with a spoon laid neatly beside it. Again I felt the guilt and quickly ate my soup, which had gone cold. I went upstairs hoping to apologize to Mother, only to find her asleep. Not wanting to disturb her, I walked back to my room, footsteps heavy, and fell into a deep slumber.

Chapter 3

The Day the Sky Came Crashing Down

The days went by as slow as dripping molasses, one day after the other. We barely ventured out of the house, with the exception of a few trips to the town market. Mother fell into a kind of work phase. She dusted, washed, and polished everything. Not a single insect dared step in our house. Clothes were organized, every nook and cranny was scrubbed, and all kitchen utensils were organized from largest to smallest. When I asked about the cleaning, she had said, "I couldn't help noticing how dirty everything was recently. Besides, that way your father can come home to a clean house." But I knew she was worried.

On a Wednesday, we decided to visit the local library. Mother, toting her heavy belly, put on her nice sun hat and a bright yellow maternity dress. Dressed up, Mother looked more like her put-together self. And I, who was so glad to have a reason to get out of the house, wore one of my favorite white dresses with small roses embroidered into the fabric.

As we walked down the streets full of people, I started to slouch and looked at my feet.

"Look up, Lily," said Mother. "And straighten your posture."

I did what was asked grudgingly, feeling noticeably more vulnerable. When it was too overwhelming, I slid behind Mother where she couldn't see me and resumed my crunched up pose.

We walked through the grand entrance of the library, and immediately the noise and commotion of the streets began to die down. The library held tall cedar shelves, full of books in leather covers all with the same gold script. Mother and I each chose a book and headed home.

As we walked, the sky was clear and the birds hummed. Flower vendors had booths overflowing with blooms. I couldn't help but shake free of my worry and enjoy the scenes, but my moment of bliss soon diminished when I saw a boy on a bike turning into our street. The boy rode around the town every day delivering the bad news to the families of soldiers.

"You don't think we will get any news, do you?" I asked Mother.

"No, no, I'm sure he is just going through our street to get to the next. Don't worry," Mother replied, but her face was pinched with worry, and she quickened her pace.

Cold sweat ran down my back. I could tell the bike boy was nearing our house now.

Mother, sensing my impatience, said, "You can run. I'll be fine."

As soon as the words left her mouth, I broke into a sprint. It wasn't a very ladylike thing to do, but, at that moment, I didn't care.

I heard the pounding in my ears every time my feet hit the pavement.

My mouth felt dry, and I was having a hard time breathing.

I could see the boy more clearly now, and I was hoping, praying for him to pass our house.

But my prayers were not answered,

and the boy halted just outside our
door. I crumpled to the sidewalk,
not processing that it was actual-
ly happening. I had so much hope,
everything was supposed to go as
planned. I was supposed to win the
game, have a happily-ever-after.

Everything was a blur, nausea
swept over me, and I had trouble hear-
ing. Mother came, she talked to the
boy. She was crying, she never cried.

I couldn't move, the boy came and
crouched by me, I could feel his hand
on my shoulder.

"I'm sorry, Miss."

I fainted right there and then.

Honor Roll

Welcome to the *Stone Soup* Honor Roll. Every month we receive submissions from hundreds of kids from around the world. Unfortunately, we don't have space to publish all the great work we receive. We want to commend some of these talented writers and artists and encourage them to keep creating.

Fiction
Reiyah Jacobs, 13
Ella Jeon, 11
Lissa Krueger, 11
Haeon Lee, 11
Grace Malary McAndrew, 12

Poetry
Gia Bharadwaj, 12
Rhône Galchen, 11
Harry Kavanaugh, 10
Uma Nambiar, 11
Billy Ren, 11
Christina Smyth, 11

Art
Catherine Gruen, 12
Natalie Johnson, 13
Sarah Pledger, 12
Sophia Torres, 11
Calci Wolfe, 13

Visit the *Stone Soup* store at Stonesoupstore.com to buy:

- Magazines—individual issues of *Stone Soup*, past and present

- Books—our collection of themed anthologies (fantasy, sport, poetry, and more), and the *Stone Soup Annual* (all the year's issues, plus a taste of the year online, in one volume)

- Art prints—high quality prints from our collection of children's art

- Journals and sketchbooks for writing and drawing

. . . and more!

Don't forget to visit Stonesoup.com to browse our bonus materials. There you will find:

- 20 years of back issues—around 5,000 stories, poems, and reviews

- Blog posts from our young bloggers on subjects from sports to sewing—plus ecology, reading, and book reviews

- Video interviews with *Stone Soup* authors

- Music, spoken word, and performances

CPSIA information can be obtained
at www.ICGtesting.com
Printed in the USA
LVHW020221290319
612239LV00002B/2/P